CONTENTS

OPEN SEASON

ANNUAL 2007

Pedigree®

Published by Pedigree Books Limited
Beech Hill House, Walnut Gardens, Exeter, Devon EX4 4DH.
E-mail books@pedigreegroup.co.uk
Published 2006

£6.99

MEET THE CHARACTERS

BOO

ELLIOT

ELLIOT IS A SCRAWNY, FAST-TALKING MULE DEER WHO ARRIVES IN TIMBERLINE STRAPPED TO THE BONNET OF A TRUCK AND MISSING AN ANTLER, COURTESY OF THE HUNTER SHAW. AS THE RUNT OF THE FOREST, ELLIOT COMES ACROSS AS BEING A PEST, BUT ALL HE REALLY WANTS IS TO BE ACCEPTED. AFTER HE PERSUADES BOOG TO UNTIE HIM, NEITHER OF THEIR LIVES WILL EVER BE THE SAME AGAIN.

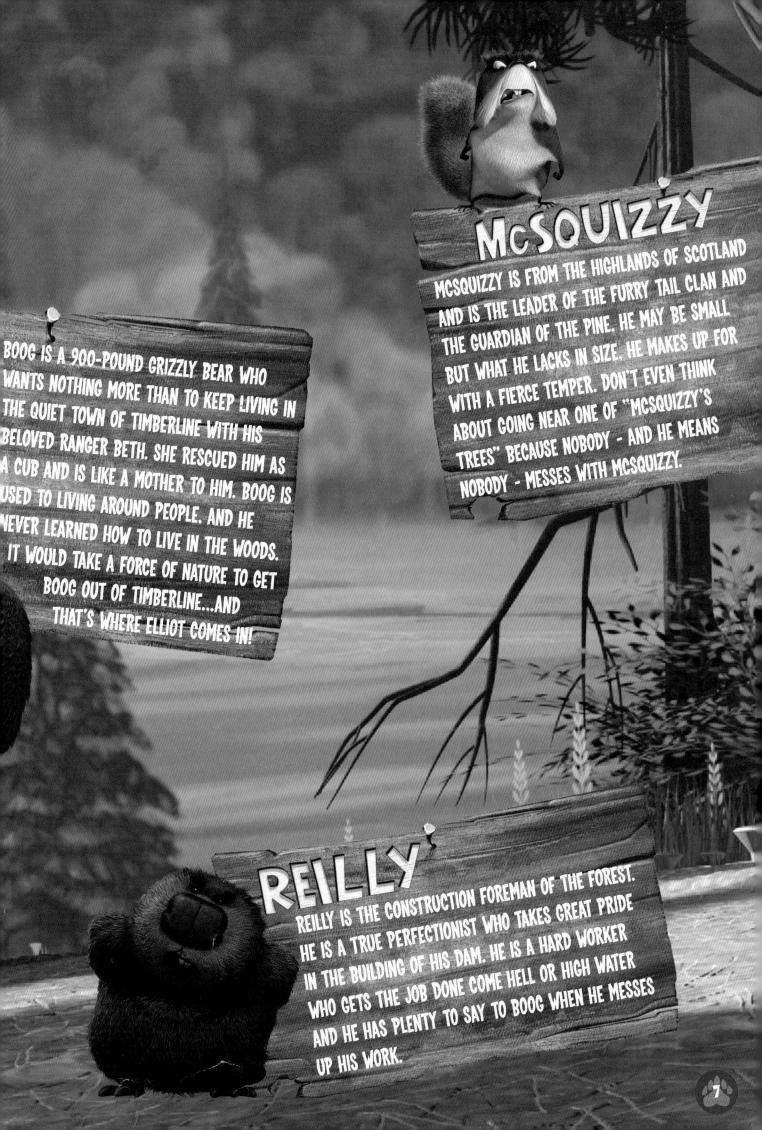

BOOG IS A 900-POUND GRIZZLY BEAR WHO WANTS NOTHING MORE THAN TO KEEP LIVING IN THE QUIET TOWN OF TIMBERLINE WITH HIS BELOVED RANGER BETH. SHE RESCUED HIM AS A CUB AND IS LIKE A MOTHER TO HIM. BOOG IS USED TO LIVING AROUND PEOPLE, AND HE NEVER LEARNED HOW TO LIVE IN THE WOODS. IT WOULD TAKE A FORCE OF NATURE TO GET BOOG OUT OF TIMBERLINE...AND THAT'S WHERE ELLIOT COMES IN!

McSQUIZZY

MCSQUIZZY IS FROM THE HIGHLANDS OF SCOTLAND AND IS THE LEADER OF THE FURRY TAIL CLAN AND THE GUARDIAN OF THE PINE. HE MAY BE SMALL BUT WHAT HE LACKS IN SIZE, HE MAKES UP FOR WITH A FIERCE TEMPER. DON'T EVEN THINK ABOUT GOING NEAR ONE OF "MCSQUIZZY'S TREES" BECAUSE NOBODY - AND HE MEANS NOBODY - MESSES WITH MCSQUIZZY.

REILLY

REILLY IS THE CONSTRUCTION FOREMAN OF THE FOREST. HE IS A TRUE PERFECTIONIST WHO TAKES GREAT PRIDE IN THE BUILDING OF HIS DAM. HE IS A HARD WORKER WHO GETS THE JOB DONE COME HELL OR HIGH WATER AND HE HAS PLENTY TO SAY TO BOOG WHEN HE MESSES UP HIS WORK.

DENI AND SERG
THE PSYCHO DUCKS

THESE TWO "QUACKPOTS" HAVE BEEN SHOT AT ONE TOO MANY TIMES, FLED IN TOO MANY MIGRATIONS AND NOW JUST REFUSE TO FLY. EVENTUALLY THE SHELL-SHOCKED PAIR GET THEIR CHANCE FOR PAYBACK WHEN BOOG AND ELLIOT ENLIST THEIR HELP TO WARD OFF THE HUNTER. SHAW AND THE OTHERS.

MARIA AND ROSIE

YOU DO NOT WANT TO MESS WITH THESE TWO LADIES. IF YOU DARE TO B[?] AROUND THEM. YOU HAD BETTER WATCH OUT. BECAUSE THEIR HOT TEMPERS ARE PEPPERED WITH A SALSA FLAVOUR AND A SASSY COMEBACK EVERY TIME. SO ALL YOU HUNTERS OUT THERE. REMEMBER. YOU CAN RUN, BUT YOU CAN'T HIDE.

PORCUPINE (BUDDY)

IT'S DIFFICULT TO GET CLOSE TO SOMEONE WHO IS SO PRICKLY, WHICH IS REALLY SAD BECAUSE THIS LONER IS IN CONSTANT SEARCH FOR A HUG. HE DOESN'T UNDERSTAND THAT PEOPLE WON'T HUG HIM BECAUSE HE'S DOWNRIGHT PAINFUL TO BE AROUND.

MR. WEENIE

A DOMESTICATED DACHSHUND ACCUSTOMED TO THE PAMPERED GOOD LIFE. HE HAS A PERSONALITY TO MATCH HIS NAME. BUT WHEN HE IS TAKEN CAPTIVE BY THE FURRY TAIL CLAN, HE DISCOVERS THAT HIS WHOLE LIFE HAS BEEN A LIE.

BOOG, MEET ELLIOT

Nestled in the mighty Sawtooth Mountains, Timberline is a small, sleepy mountain community with one main street. It's home to Ranger Beth and her 900lb domesticated grizzly bear Boog.

Shaw, the meanest, mullet-headed, snaggle-toothed hunter in Timberline came roaring down the street with a scrawny, one-horned Mule Deer strapped to the bonnet of his truck. He strolled into the Fish and Game Office. Just then Ranger Beth and Boog arrived. Beth took one look at the poor deer and stormed into the office after Shaw.

"Cuff him Gordy!" fumed Beth to the Sheriff, "He's at it again!" Through the window, Gordy spotted the deer on Shaw's truck.

"Shaw, hunting season doesn't start for three days. What are you doing with that buck on your hood?" asked Gordy sternly.

"What? It ain't my fault, he ran right in front of my truck" replied Shaw

Outside the office, Boog was waiting impatiently in Beth's jeep. "Where is that Girl? Never mind, I may as well get some shut eye". Boog started to go to sleep when a strange noise woke him. He sat bolt upright and looked around. He moved closer to the deer. "Phew, that's nasty" he said as he got a whiff of the deer. Suddenly, the deer woke up. "Ahhhh!" screamed Boog. "Ahhhh!" screamed the deer.

"What the...what's going on? Where am I? I saw two bright lights."
Boog composed himself and tried to play it cool. "No, you're not dead yet, but seeing as that is Shaw's truck..."
"What's a Shaw?" asks the deer.
"Only the nastiest hunter in town".
"A hunter! Did he get you too?
Boog chuckled to himself at the idea of him being hunted like a woodland animal.
"Nobody's hunting this bear".

"Well then, untie me? Please, no one is looking!" begged the deer.
Boog shook his head. "Ain't gonna be able to do it". The deer burst into tears.
"What am I gonna do? I don't want to be mounted on a wall!"
"Calm down", said Boog "It's not going to happen with that rack."

"I don't have a problem with my..." Just then the deer caught a glimpse of himself in the truck's mirror. He had lost one of his horns.
"AAAUUUUGHHHHH! My...It's...Wha...? I'm a UNIHORN! Don't look at me! I'm hideous! I'm a monster!"
Sobbing, the deer dropped his head on to the bonnet of the truck with a thump.

Just then Beth came out of the office and got back into her car. Boog was glad to be getting away from the weird deer and all his whining.
"Come on, I'm begging you. Please, please! Just untie me! Come on...please, please, please!"
Boog couldn't take it anymore, so he leant over and cut the deer free with one swish of his claw.

DON'T FEED THE BEARS!

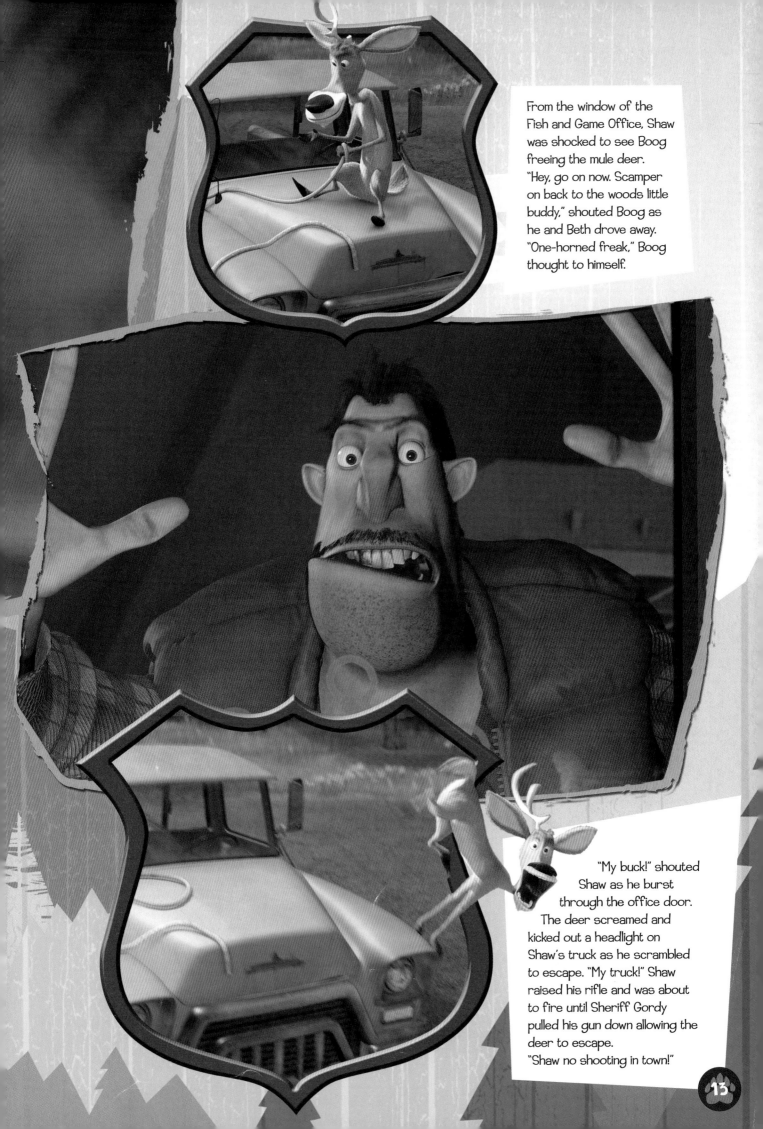

From the window of the Fish and Game Office, Shaw was shocked to see Boog freeing the mule deer. "Hey, go on now. Scamper on back to the woods little buddy," shouted Boog as he and Beth drove away. "One-horned freak," Boog thought to himself.

"My buck!" shouted Shaw as he burst through the office door. The deer screamed and kicked out a headlight on Shaw's truck as he scrambled to escape. "My truck!" Shaw raised his rifle and was about to fire until Sheriff Gordy pulled his gun down allowing the deer to escape. "Shaw no shooting in town!"

Later that night, back at Beth's house, Boog was in his garage watching *Wheel of Fortune* on his TV.
"Ok buddy, time for bed" said Beth as turned off the TV. Boog grumbled and turned the TV back on.
"Boog" said Beth sternly as she turned the TV off again "Mr. Dinkelman's waiting" as she gestured to a small teddy bear in Boog's bed.

Boog ambled over to his bed and settled in. "Good night big guy!" said Beth as she was leaving. Boog looked up expectantly and started to whimper.
"Oh did I forget something" asked Beth as she pulled a fish-shaped biscuit out of her pocket.
Boog swallowed the biscuit in one big gulp and made a puppy dog face, begging for another.
"No no, no more treats for you. Stop it Boog. Not the face. Oh you're so cute". Beth couldn't resist giving Boog just one more treat.
"Oh alright, but that's it. Now go to sleep. Good night Boog". Boog snuggled up with Mr. Dinkelman and went to sleep.

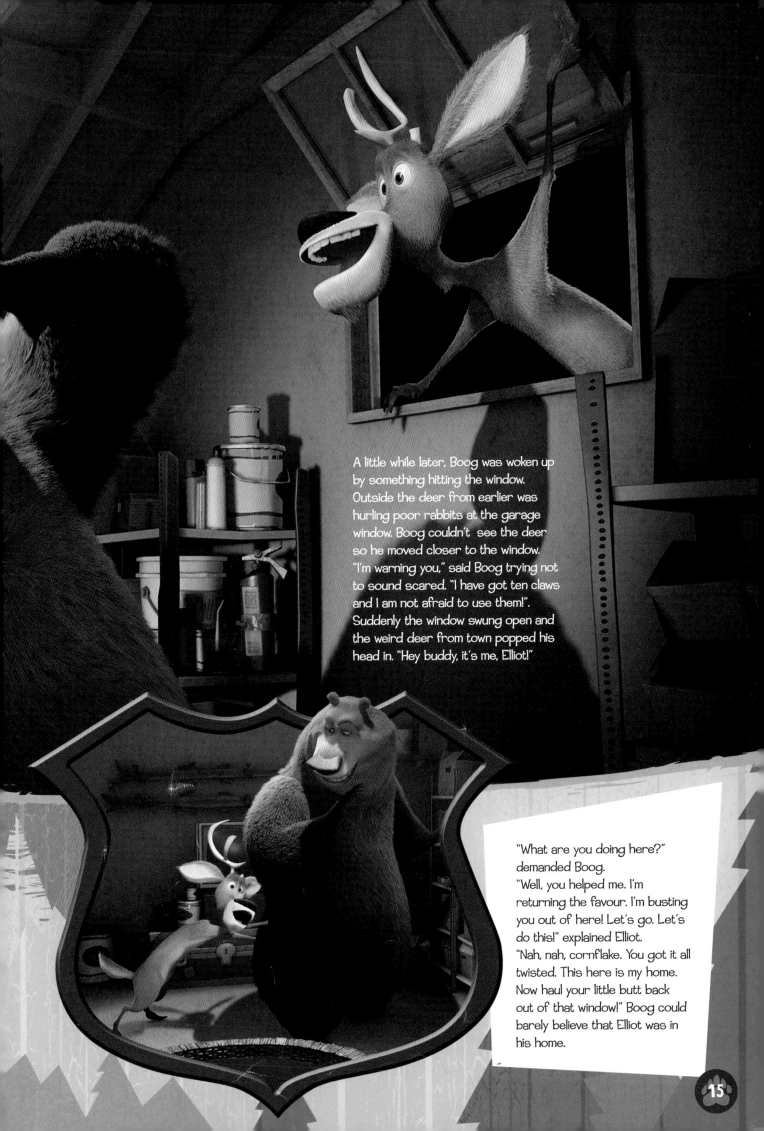

A little while later, Boog was woken up by something hitting the window. Outside the deer from earlier was hurling poor rabbits at the garage window. Boog couldn't see the deer so he moved closer to the window. "I'm warning you," said Boog trying not to sound scared. "I have got ten claws and I am not afraid to use them!". Suddenly the window swung open and the weird deer from town popped his head in. "Hey buddy, it's me, Elliot!"

"What are you doing here?" demanded Boog.
"Well, you helped me. I'm returning the favour. I'm busting you out of here! Let's go. Let's do this!" explained Elliot.
"Nah, nah, cornflake. You got it all twisted. This here is my home. Now haul your little butt back out of that window!" Boog could barely believe that Elliot was in his home.

Elliot opened the garage door. "Come on, let's go!" Boog looked out into cold dark night. "Outside?" He asked nervously. "Why would I want to go outside when I got all I need in..."
Boog's nose started to twitch like it had a life of it's own. It dragged him across the garage to where Elliot was chomping on a candy bar. "What's that?" asked Boog excitedly.

"I call 'em Woo Hoo's! I know where there is a bunch of them, but you gotta come outside!"
Elliot started to tease Boog with the candy bar, jumping in and out of the garage.
Boog could not resist any longer and chomped down on the candy bar. A wave of pure happiness washed over his face.
"Woo Hoo!" cried Boog as he and Elliot snuck out into the night.

Boog and Elliot peered over a car as Elliot pointed to a Dumpster in a dark alley.
"Ok, I got that Woo Hoo right out of one of those container doo-hickies."
"You got it out of the garbage?" asked Boog disgusted. "I had that in my mouth and everything."
Boog's nose suddenly started to twitch as he noticed the PuniMart store just across the street. "It's a whole Woo Hoo villiage!"

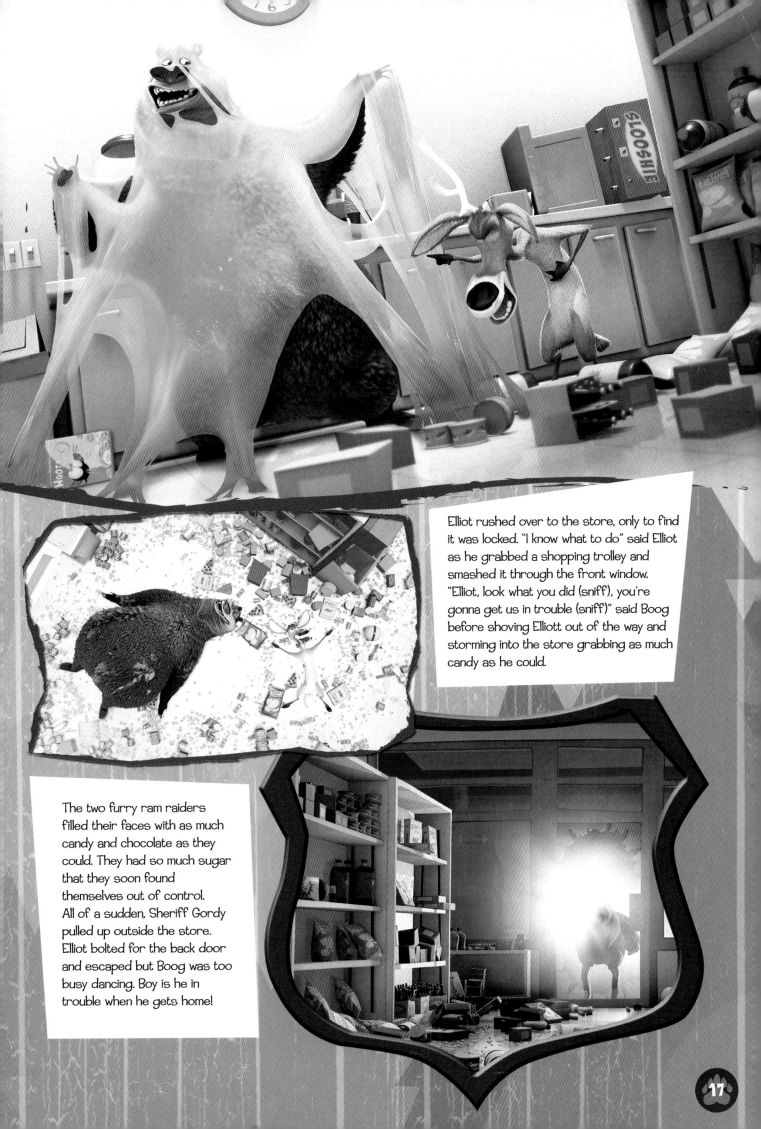

Elliot rushed over to the store, only to find it was locked. "I know what to do" said Elliot as he grabbed a shopping trolley and smashed it through the front window. "Elliot, look what you did (sniff), you're gonna get us in trouble (sniff)" said Boog before shoving Elliott out of the way and storming into the store grabbing as much candy as he could.

The two furry ram raiders filled their faces with as much candy and chocolate as they could. They had so much sugar that they soon found themselves out of control. All of a sudden, Sheriff Gordy pulled up outside the store. Elliot bolted for the back door and escaped but Boog was too busy dancing. Boy is he in trouble when he gets home!

The next day Boog was getting ready to perform at the amphitheatre in his show with Ranger Beth. The night before when he had been taken home by Sheriff Gordy, Beth had been very angry with him so he had to be on his best behaviour today. Suddenly Elliot burst in backstage. He had slept in a Dumpster all night and had been spotted by Hunter Shaw that morning. "Hide me!" cried Elliot.

"No way! You have gotten me into enough trouble already" replied Boog.

The show was about to start and Boog really did not want to deal with Elliot. "Ok get out!" roared Boog.

Elliot ran from behind the curtain on to the stage. All the people watching the show thought it was a joke. They had come to see a grizzly bear, not a deer! "You're ruining my show" growled Boog as he jumped on to the stage and attacked Elliot.

The audience were getting scared now. All they could see was a big angry bear fighting with a poor little dear.

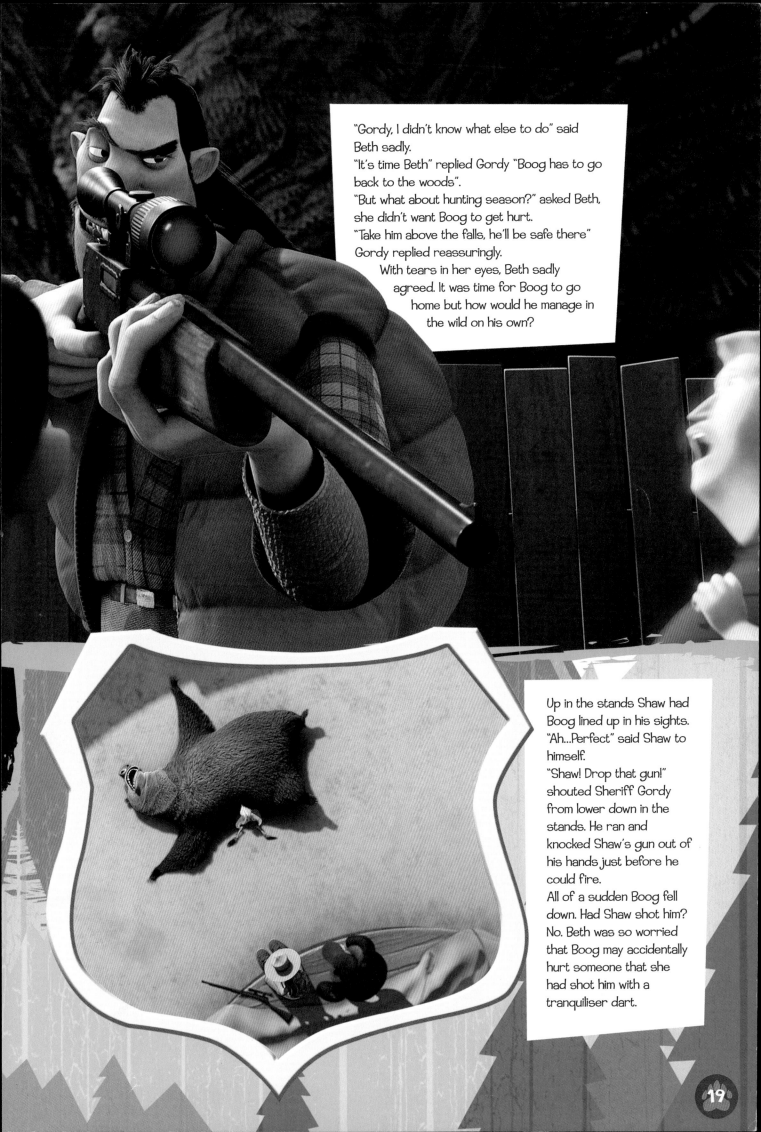

"Gordy, I didn't know what else to do" said Beth sadly.

"It's time Beth" replied Gordy "Boog has to go back to the woods".

"But what about hunting season?" asked Beth, she didn't want Boog to get hurt.

"Take him above the falls, he'll be safe there" Gordy replied reassuringly.

With tears in her eyes, Beth sadly agreed. It was time for Boog to go home but how would he manage in the wild on his own?

Up in the stands Shaw had Boog lined up in his sights.

"Ah...Perfect" said Shaw to himself.

"Shaw! Drop that gun!" shouted Sheriff Gordy from lower down in the stands. He ran and knocked Shaw's gun out of his hands just before he could fire.

All of a sudden Boog fell down. Had Shaw shot him? No. Beth was so worried that Boog may accidentally hurt someone that she had shot him with a tranquiliser dart.

19

MATCH THE TRACKS

Every breed of animal leaves different tracks in the forest. See if you can correctly guess which tracks belong to which animal and draw a line to link them. Then check the answers at the bottom of the page to see if you are right.

1.) THESE PAW PRINTS BELONG TO SOMETHING BIG AND HEAVY, WITH CLAWS GOOD FOR CLIMBING TREES.

2.) THESE SMALL NIMBLE PAWS CAN CLIMB AND GRIP VERY WELL.

3.) THESE WIDE WEBBED FEET MEAN A BORN SWIMMER.

4.) THESE LONG STRONG WEEBED FEET ARE GOOD IN WATER AS WELL AS ON LAND.

ANSWERS: 1.) BEAR, 2.) SQUIRREL, 3.) DUCK, 4.) BEAVER.

BACK TO TIMBERLINE

Can you help Boog and Mr. Dinkelman find their way out of the woods and back to Timberline? Be careful, it's hunting season and Shaw is in hot pursuit.

TIMBERLINE

INTO THE WOODS

The next day Boog woke up to find himself in the middle of the wilderness. Ranger Beth had dropped him off the night before while he was still tranquilised. Worse than that though, Elliot was still with him.
"Take a good look Elliot! What do you see? Something is missing, what is it Elliot? What is it?" Boog cried desperately. "Timberline is missing! My garage is missing, breakfast, lunch and dinner are missing...My whole life is missing. AND IT'S ALL YOUR FAULT!"
"I was just going to say that" replied Elliot.

"I have got to get home," Boog thought to himself, "she was angry but I will be able to sort it out, I just need to get home".
Boog thought that if he could just get his bearings then he would be able to find his way back to Timberline. He looked up at the nearest tree. "I could climb that and see which way home is," he thought.

Just then Boog heard a strange voice coming from the very top of the tree. "This is McSquizzy's turf and no one messes with McSquizzy, 'cause that's me. Touch a needle on this tree and I'll give you such a doin'!"

"Yeah!? You and what army" Boog shouted back up the tree. McSquizzy let out a loud whistle and hundreds of squirrels appeared around him.

"Oh, that army," said Boog under his breath.

"OUCH!" Out of nowhere an acorn hit Boog on the head. "That's it! You're asking for a whoopin'". Boog made a final grab for the tree but before he could start to climb a barrage of acorns rained down onto him covering him from head to toe.

Boog realised that if he was going to get out of the woods he was going to have to rely on the very deer that had gotten him into this mess... Elliot.

23

Boog and Elliot agreed to be partners and get out of the forest. Elliot led Boog through the trees in the direction he thought would take them back to Timberline.

"Ok, forest lesson 1," Elliot started, "these big, wood stick things are called trees". Elliot bounded effortlessly up the side of a mountain with Boog struggling behind. "The big rocks are called mountains and the little rocks are their babies" explained Elliot, oblivious to Boog who was barely hanging on.

Suddenly Boog lost his grip and started to slide down the mountain.

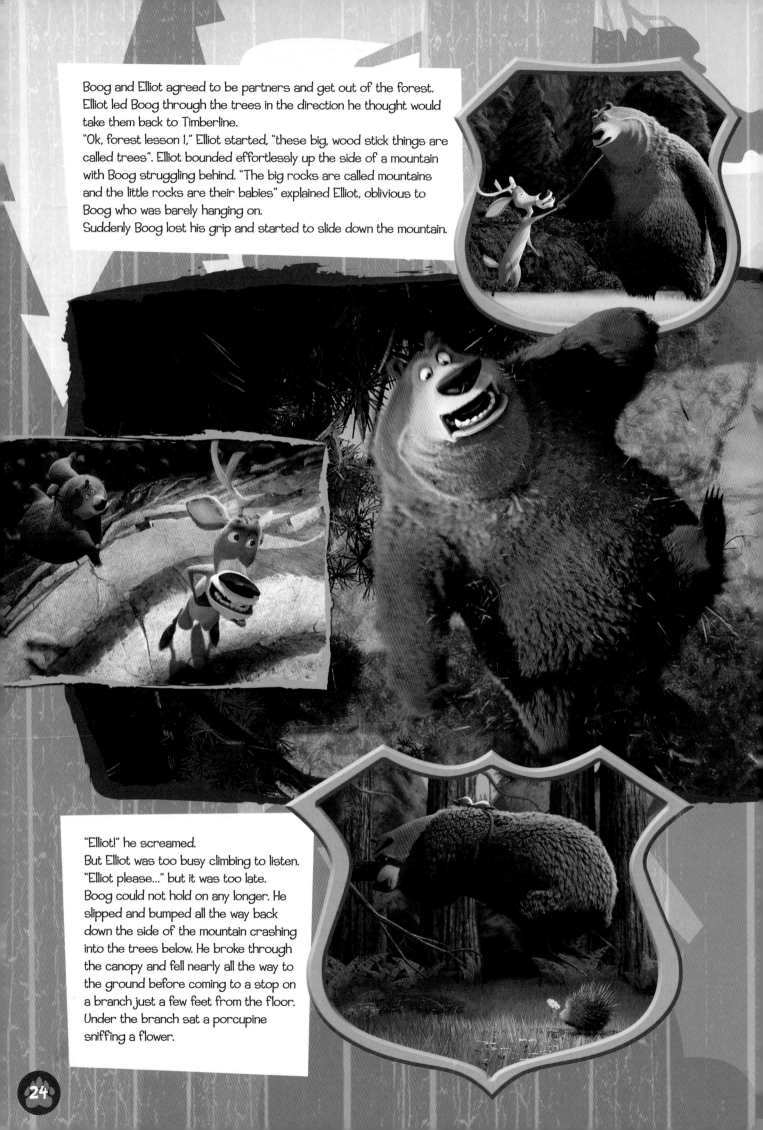

"Elliot!" he screamed.

But Elliot was too busy climbing to listen.

"Elliot please..." but it was too late.

Boog could not hold on any longer. He slipped and bumped all the way back down the side of the mountain crashing into the trees below. He broke through the canopy and fell nearly all the way to the ground before coming to a stop on a branch just a few feet from the floor. Under the branch sat a porcupine sniffing a flower.

Boog could feel the branch creaking under his weight. All of a sudden it snapped and he landed butt first on top of the porcupine.

"Ahhhhh!" screamed Boog.

Elliot came rushing back down the mountain to see what all the noise was about. As you can imagine, he found the whole thing pretty funny. Elliot made Boog lay down on a rock so that he could pull the prickly porcupine off his butt.

"Just rip it off fast like a bandage." shouted Boog.

"Hold still! Okay...just be calm, this might pinch a little" said Elliot, not to Boog but to the porcupine.

"Just get it over with!" screamed Boog who by now was in quite a lot of pain. Elliot spat on his hooves and took hold of the little porcupine. With an almighty yank he ripped the small creature off of Boog's big behind.

Boog let out a scream that could be heard across the whole of the forest!

25

Boog and Elliot carried on deeper into the forest. They came across a river where a group of beavers were building a dam. The beavers were sitting down to their lunch of wood when Reilly, the Construction Foreman, noticed Boog and Elliot walking by. "Hey, hey guys, check it out. The largest carnivore in North America, the mighty grizzly". Boog and Elliot kept on walking. After seeing the beavers having their lunch, Boog realised that it had been ages since he had eaten anything.

"I'm starving" Boog said to Elliot.
"Here eat this" replied Elliot tossing Boog a pine cone.
"I can't eat that, bears don't eat pine cones!"
"What do you eat then" asked Elliot.
For a moment Boog was not sure, Beth had always made his meals for him.
"Ummm...ah...FISH!" Boog said, very proudly.
So Boog headed down to the side of the river.
"Ok fishies, give it up for Boog".
Just as Boog finished speaking three salmon leapt from the water.
"HI YAA!" they cried as they karate kicked Boog in the face with their tails.

After failing to catch any fish, Boog and Elliot continued through the trees with Boog chewing on a pine cone.
"Hey Elliot, I need the toilet" said Boog.
Elliot stared blankly back. Being a woodland creature he did not know what a toilet was.
"Don't look now, but I see a little bush over there with your name on it," said Elliot.
"A bush?! Are you serious" gasped Boog, but there was no where else to go. Boog headed over to the bush and sat down, trying to get comfortable. Suddenly a pair of skunks appeared at Boog's feet. These were no ordinary skunks, they were Maria and Rosie.

"What are you doing on my house?" demanded Maria.
"Your house? Sorry, I did not know" replied Boog a little embarrassed.
"It would probably be an improvement" sniggered Rosie. The two skunks started to argue. Boog was not sure what to do.
"Show 'em who's boss" suggested Elliot "Mark your territory!"
"All right ladies, I'm laying down the law..." started Boog, but before he could finish his sentence the two skunks' tails snapped to attention and sprayed their icky stink right in Boog's face.

Meanwhile, Elliot had spotted a member of his old herd, Giselle. Elliot has had a crush on Giselle since the first moment he saw her, but he had never had the confidence to tell her because of another deer, the leader of the herd, Ian. Ian made Elliot's life miserable when he was in the herd. Ian was the big buck. He ran the herd and picked on Elliot every chance he got.

"I think you had better get out of here" said Giselle, "You know what happened last time". Suddenly thirty deer rose up out of the grass in a perfect line. Elliot was confronted by his whole herd, including Ian.
"What are you doing here Smelliot?" chortled Ian, "I thought I told you to leave the herd and never ever come back?"
With an almighty CRACK! Ian punched Elliot with his horns sending him flying into the air.
"Arrrghhh!" cried Elliot.

Hearing Elliot's cries, Boog finishes cleaning off the skunk smell and charges towards the noise.

"Roar!!!!" growled Boog, scaring all the deer.

"Bear. Bear. It's a bear" shrieked Ian, scared out of his wits. As Boog helped Elliot back to his feet one of the deer noticed Mr. Dinkelman, Boog's teddy, strapped to his back.

"Oh," laughed Ian, "I've heard of you. You're that bear who got his butt thumped by a squirrel. Ha!"

All the other deer started laughing at Boog. They obviously were not scared of him anymore.

"Boog, what's that short for?" asked Ian, "Booger?!"

Boog and Elliot tried to leave but Ian got right up in their faces.

"You two are perfect for each other," he started. "You're a loser and you're a loser-er! Herd, let's bound!"

With that all of the deer trotted off back into the forest. All except Giselle who stayed behind to say goodbye to Elliot.

"Maybe it will grow back," she said looking at Elliot's broken horn. "Bye Elliot."

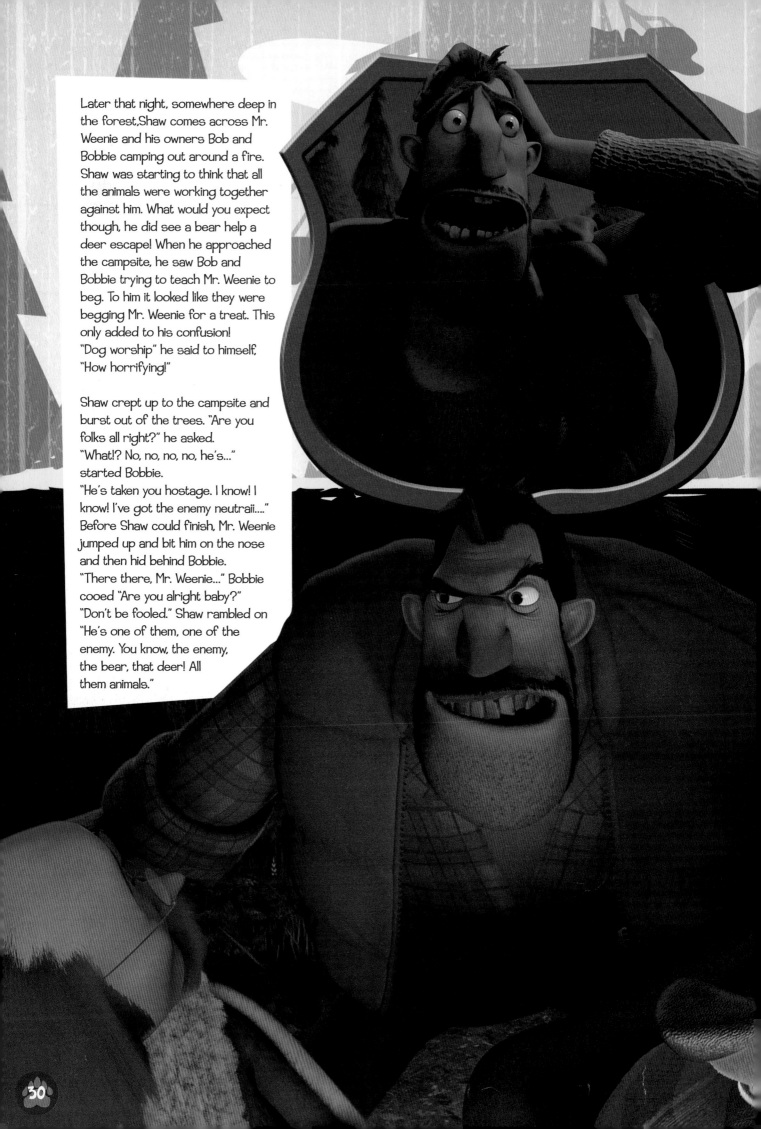

Later that night, somewhere deep in the forest,Shaw comes across Mr. Weenie and his owners Bob and Bobbie camping out around a fire. Shaw was starting to think that all the animals were working together against him. What would you expect though, he did see a bear help a deer escape! When he approached the campsite, he saw Bob and Bobbie trying to teach Mr. Weenie to beg. To him it looked like they were begging Mr. Weenie for a treat. This only added to his confusion!
"Dog worship" he said to himself, "How horrifying!"

Shaw crept up to the campsite and burst out of the trees. "Are you folks all right?" he asked.
"What!? No, no, no, no, he's..." started Bobbie.
"He's taken you hostage. I know! I know! I've got the enemy neutraii...." Before Shaw could finish, Mr. Weenie jumped up and bit him on the nose and then hid behind Bobbie.
"There there, Mr. Weenie..." Bobbie cooed "Are you alright baby?"
"Don't be fooled." Shaw rambled on "He's one of them, one of the enemy. You know, the enemy, the bear, that deer! All them animals."

Shaw continued in a crazed manner,
"I've seen the future. If I don't stop them it will be a
total reversal of the natural order! Animals will be
driving around in cars while we are walked on leashes."
By now Bob and Bobbie were wide eyed with terror.
"Back in Timberline, they laugh at old Shaw,
but you'll see, the truth will be revealed."

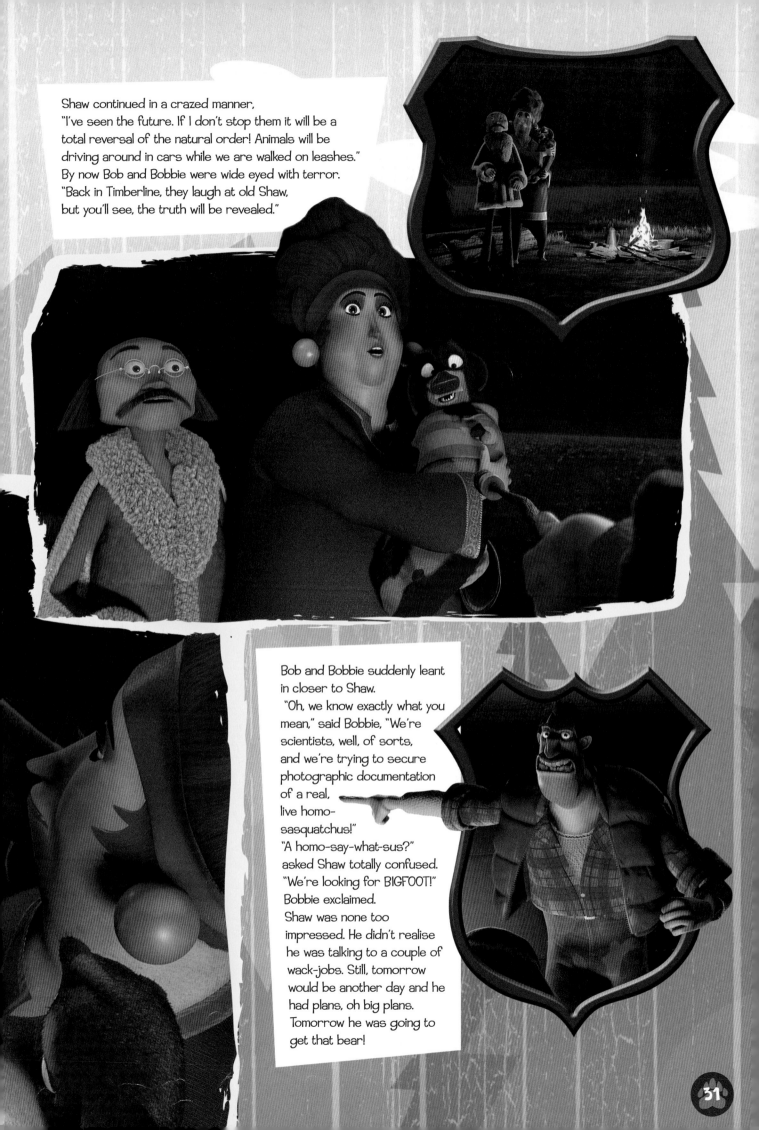

Bob and Bobbie suddenly leant
in closer to Shaw.
"Oh, we know exactly what you
mean," said Bobbie, "We're
scientists, well, of sorts,
and we're trying to secure
photographic documentation
of a real,
live homo-
sasquatchus!"
"A homo-say-what-sus?"
asked Shaw totally confused.
"We're looking for BIGFOOT!"
Bobbie exclaimed.
Shaw was none too
impressed. He didn't realise
he was talking to a couple of
wack-jobs. Still, tomorrow
would be another day and he
had plans, oh big plans.
Tomorrow he was going to
get that bear!

HIDE

HOW TO PLAY

CAN YOU FIND YOUR WAY THROUGH THE WOODS WITHOUT RUNNING INTO SHAW? ROLL THE DICE AND MOVE YOUR COUNTER. IF YOU LAND ON A LOG, CLIMB UP IT TO GET AHEAD. BE CAREFUL THOUGH BECAUSE IF YOU LAND ON SHAW'S SQUARE, YOU HAVE TO GO RIGHT BACK TO THE START!

29 30 31

28 27 26

15 16 17

14 13 12

1 2 3

START

FROM THE HUNTER

OPEN SEASON™
WORD SEARCH

Can you find all the words hidden in this Word Search? If you can then maybe you should be helping Boog find his way out of the woods!

G	P	G	Z	I	Y	R	S	G	L	E	M
W	O	O	P	L	E	L	I	I	N	X	C
J	U	Q	R	W	I	S	L	I	O	Y	S
F	U	R	A	C	E	M	L	I	B	D	Q
H	W	H	P	L	U	R	O	I	E	F	U
L	S	T	L	X	E	P	G	B	U	R	I
T	D	E	U	B	Y	A	I	G	O	I	Z
O	Y	M	M	B	O	O	G	N	F	O	Z
I	C	I	T	S	E	R	O	F	E	W	Y
L	T	R	A	N	G	E	R	B	E	T	H
L	P	B	S	Q	W	A	X	Y	E	K	Z
E	Y	T	E	S	B	T	G	K	M	F	Y

| BOOG | FOREST | MCSQUIZZY | RANGERBETH | SHAW |
| ELLIOT | GISELLE | PORCUPINE | REILLY | TIMBERLINE |

34

CROSSWORD

ACROSS

2 THE MEANEST HUNTER IN TIMBERLINE
4 HE IS THE BOSS AT THE DAM
5 HE MAKES SURE EVERYONE OBEYS THE LAW
6 SHE REALLY MISSES BOOG
8 BOB AND BOBBIE'S DOG

DOWN

1 BOOG REALLY LIKES TO EAT THIS
3 ALL HE WANTS IS A HUG BUT HE'S TOO SPIKY
5 ELLIOT HAS HAD A CRUSH ON HER FOR YEARS
6 HE'S BROWN AND WEARS A TEDDY BEAR BACKPACK
7 ELLIOT IS MISSING ONE OF THESE

THE HUNTERS ARE COMING

The next morning Boog and Elliot were still making their way through the forest. All of a sudden they came across the same pair of skunks from the day before. The two of them are still arguing so Elliot and Boog paid no attention to them and kept walking. A little while later they came across a dam. Boog grabbed Elliot by the antler suspecting that they have been walking in circles. "Aren't those the same beavers" he growled. "No" replied Elliot. "All beavers look the same!" By now the beavers had spotted Boog and Elliot and started to laugh at them.

"Elliot!" growled Boog angrily "This is the same dang dam. We have been walking in circles!" KAAABLAM! From high on a hill Hunter Shaw had just fired a shot at them.
"Wahoo!" shouted Shaw excitedly "Got 'em now."
"Boog, we have to get out of here!" cried Elliot.
"I'm out of here" replied Boog already running across the dam.
"Boog wait!" shouted Elliot after his hairy friend "Don't go out there!"
But it was too late, Boog was already in the middle of the dam and it started to creak!

Before Boog could do anything the whole of the dam collapsed with a giant whoosh, taking Boog, Elliot and Reilly with it. "Arrghhhh!" they all screamed as they were carried down stream by the torrent of water. Further along the dry river bed, Ian's herd were grazing when from out of nowhere, a wall of water engulfed them.

Shaw was following on the mountain roads trying to get ahead of them. He pulled his truck into the path of the water, not really thinking about what might happen.

Within seconds his truck was being swept along by the rapids. It was all he could do to roll up his window before the water got into his truck. Groggy from the impact he turned to look out of his windscreen only to see a beaver staring back at him, then a skunk floated by and finally Boog and Elliot.

Elliot managed to climb up onto a log that was floating down river with them He pulled Boog up onto the log with him. "You're gonna be okay!" exclaimed Elliot.
"We're gonna die and you know it!" replied an exhausted Boog.
Behind them Shaw's truck broke through the surface of the water like a breaching whale!
"Ha Ha!" cried Shaw excitedly, gunning his engine and driving though the water towards them. Shaw's truck hit a huge boulder, flying up in the air and then disappearing back under the water.

"Where is he?" asked Boog.
"There he is! "replied Elliot as he spotted Shaw's truck in front of them. Shaw crawled out of his window and on to the top of his truck. He took aim with his rifle and fired. KAABLAM! He missed them. He aimed again.
"Like fishing and hunting at the same time" he snarled.
Now he had them in his sights, a perfect shot. KAABLAM! He fired, but just as he did so, Boog and Elliot vanished.

Just as Shaw had pulled the trigger on his rifle, Boog and Elliot had slipped over the edge of a massive waterfall. "Huh?" Shaw said to himself, just before he too toppled over the edge. "Ahhhhhhh!" cried Boog and Elliot as they desperately tried to hold on to the log.
"Give me a hand Boog!" Elliot screamed as he clambered onto Boog's back. "Hold me, Boog! Come on Boog, share!"
"Stop it!" Boog shouted, barely hanging on to the log himself. "Get off me! Elliott get off me! Stop!"

From out of nowhere, Shaw appeared falling right next to them. He was still clutching to his rifle. He took aim and fired again. Click! Luckily for Boog and Elliot the rifle was empty. Shaw started to reload the rifle in mid-air but before he could fire off another round, the waterfall crashed into the valley below.

The floodwaters subsided and revealed Boog and Elliot washed up on the river bank looking like a couple of drowned rats. Shaw's truck floated by before disappearing under the water but there was no sign of Shaw.

Boog struggled to his feet and shook the water from his fur. He found that he was surrounded by all of the woodland creatures. The porcupine was stuck in a tree, the two psycho ducks, Serge and Deni were coughing up water, Ian, Giselle and the rest of Elliot's herd were all stuck in the mud.

Reilly the beaver popped up from under a log, "You did this," he shouted at Boog. "You dragged us down here into the hunting grounds." Maria the skunk was scared. "Where are we going to hide," she screamed.
"We're sitting ducks out here," quacked Serge.
"And it's open season!" squealed Porcupine.

All the animals were looking at Boog with anger. They all blamed him for their predicament.

"You know what?" snapped Boog as thunder rolled off in the distance "I'm better off alone!"
"What about us?" whimpered Porcupine.
"Us! There's no "us". You're not my problem," growled Boog as he turned to Elliot. "And you, we're done!"
"But, Boog wait..." cried Elliot.
"Done!" snarled Boog as he stormed off into the woods leaving Elliot and the others behind.

Elliot stepped forward holding on to Boog's arm. "All right, that's enough! Guys, it's not his fault."
"You're right, Elliot," said Boog pulling his arm away "It's your fault! If it weren't for you, I'd be home right now. None of this would have ever happened. You said you knew the way back home and you didn't!"
"I'm sorry Boog." said Elliot, tears welling up in his eyes, "We're still partners though right?"

As Boog stomped through the forest, alone, and still upset with Elliot and the others he came across the last thing he was expecting to see, a cabin.
"Hello, excuse me, is anyone home?" he asked as he opened the creaky door. There was no one to be found.
"Now there has to be a fridge in here somewhere," Boog said to himself.
He fumbled around in the dark for a while before bumping into something.
"This must be it!" He opened the door and leaned inside. "Woo Hoo!" Boog yelled. He had found a stash of Woo Hoo bars. Boog sat down ready to tuck into his feast of chocolate but when he did he broke the chair he was trying to sit on.
He reached over to a lamp that was sat on a small table and flicked the light on.

"AHHHH!" screamed Boog. The light revealed that he was in a hunter's cabin! All around him were stuffed animals, deer heads and other small creatures. CLICK! The handle of the door was turning. Boog realised that someone was coming home!

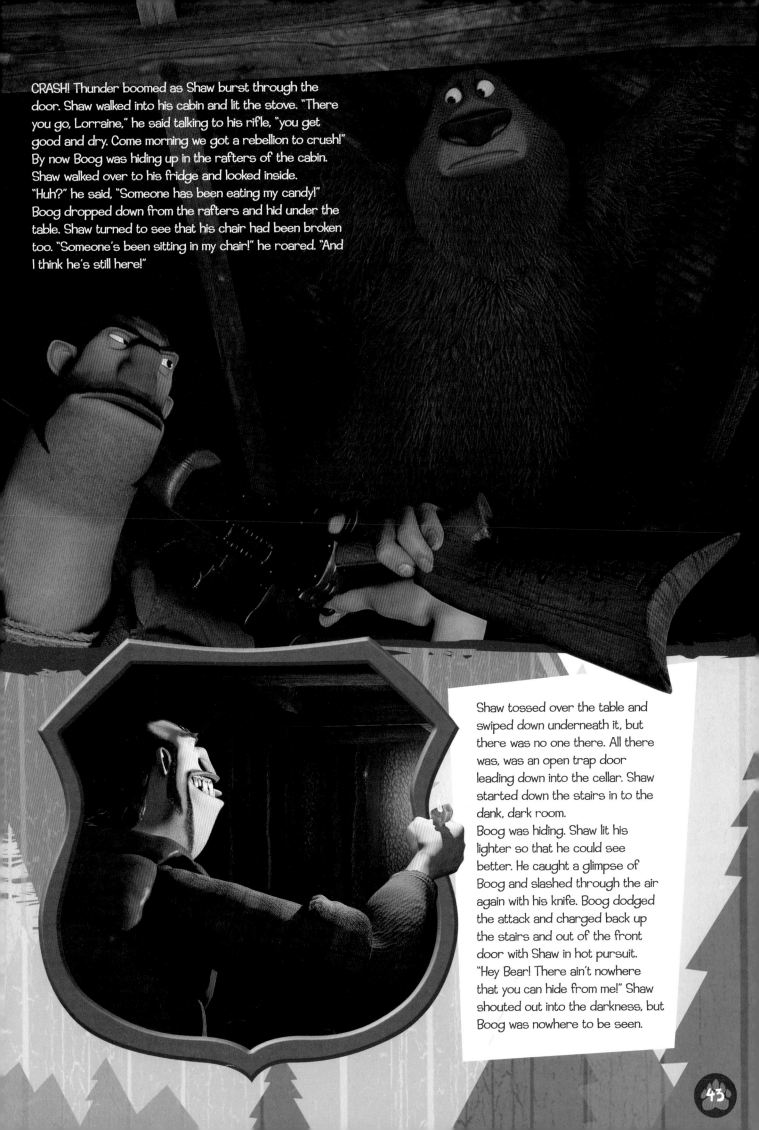

CRASH! Thunder boomed as Shaw burst through the door. Shaw walked into his cabin and lit the stove. "There you go, Lorraine," he said talking to his rifle, "you get good and dry. Come morning we got a rebellion to crush!" By now Boog was hiding up in the rafters of the cabin. Shaw walked over to his fridge and looked inside. "Huh?" he said, "Someone has been eating my candy!" Boog dropped down from the rafters and hid under the table. Shaw turned to see that his chair had been broken too. "Someone's been sitting in my chair!" he roared. "And I think he's still here!"

Shaw tossed over the table and swiped down underneath it, but there was no one there. All there was, was an open trap door leading down into the cellar. Shaw started down the stairs in to the dank, dark room.

Boog was hiding. Shaw lit his lighter so that he could see better. He caught a glimpse of Boog and slashed through the air again with his knife. Boog dodged the attack and charged back up the stairs and out of the front door with Shaw in hot pursuit. "Hey Bear! There ain't nowhere that you can hide from me!" Shaw shouted out into the darkness, but Boog was nowhere to be seen.

SPOT THE DIFFERENCE

ONE OF THESE ONE-HORNED WONDERS IS SLIGHTLY
DIFFERENT TO ALL THE OTHERS.
CAN YOU SPOT THE UNIHORN?

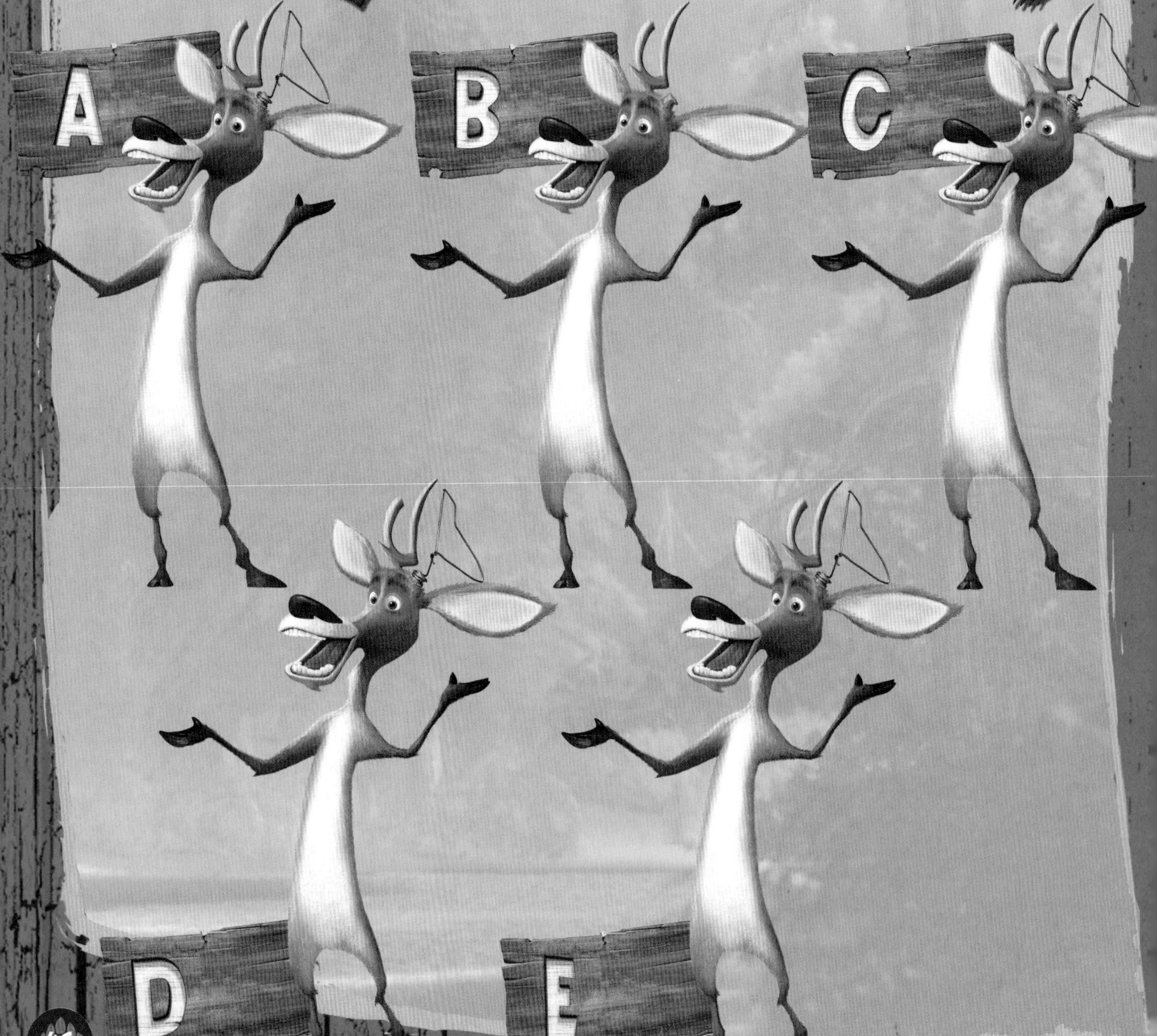

A

B

C

D

E

FIND THE CHARACTERS

CAN YOU FIND ALL THE WOODLAND CREATURES
HIDING FROM SHAW?

I BET YOU CAN'T!
THEY ARE ALL VERY GOOD
AT HIDING!

47

THE HUNTERS BECOME THE HUNTED

TIMBERLINE 5 mi

After escaping from Shaw's cabin, Boog started to think about the other animals, especially Elliot and what would happen to them if they got caught by the hunters. He decided that he would try and find them. So heading back into the woods and away from Timberline, he set off.

He soon came across the others in a little clearing hiding from the hunters who were already closing in on them.

"Boog?" said Elliot startled at the noise of Boog crashing through the woods, "What are you doing back here?"

"Come on." Boog said smiling. "I couldn't go home without my partner."

As Boog and Elliot sneak away, the other animals that had been hiding start to emerge and quietly follow them.

Boog and Elliot were sneaking from tree to tree, trying not to be spotted. Elliot thought he heard something and nervously turned around.

"Boog?" he asked "how many animals do you think would fit in the garage?

"How many what?" said Boog turning round, "WHOA!"

Behind them every animal they had met on their adventure was tip-toeing along with them!

"So you're taking us with you, right Booger!" Ian the deer cried, "I'm too pretty to get caught"
"Yeah please!" cried all the animals, "Please take us with you!" All the animals were desperate for Boog's help but there was no way they could all live in his garage. Boog backed away from all the desperate eyes staring at him. He turned to run but was stopped dead in his tracks. The way home to Timberline was blocked by dozens of flickering hunters' campfires. They were all hopelessly trapped!

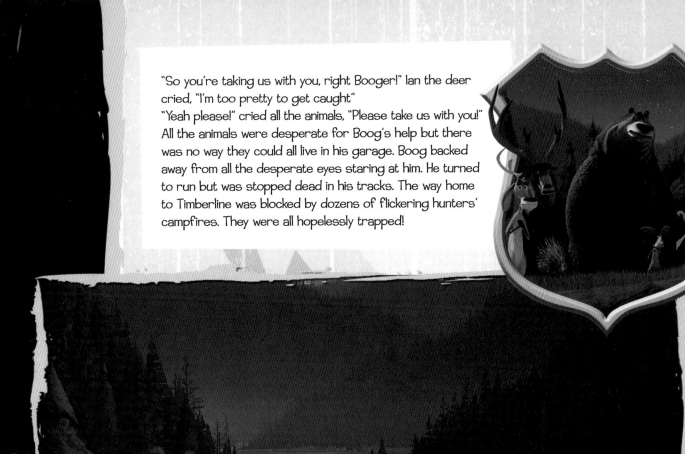

"I guess I will be mounted on a wall after all," wailed Elliot.
"No you won't!" said Boog determinedly. "I ain't going out without a fight!"
All the other animals looked confused. "That's right. If there is one thing you all have taught me it's that the woods are a dangerous place...and y'all are crazy. You've been kicking my butt for the last two days!
The animals all looked at each other and grinned in agreement.
Boog continued, "I say we do to them what you have done to me! Let's give our guests the full outdoor experience!
"Yeah!" shouted all the animals "we can do it!"

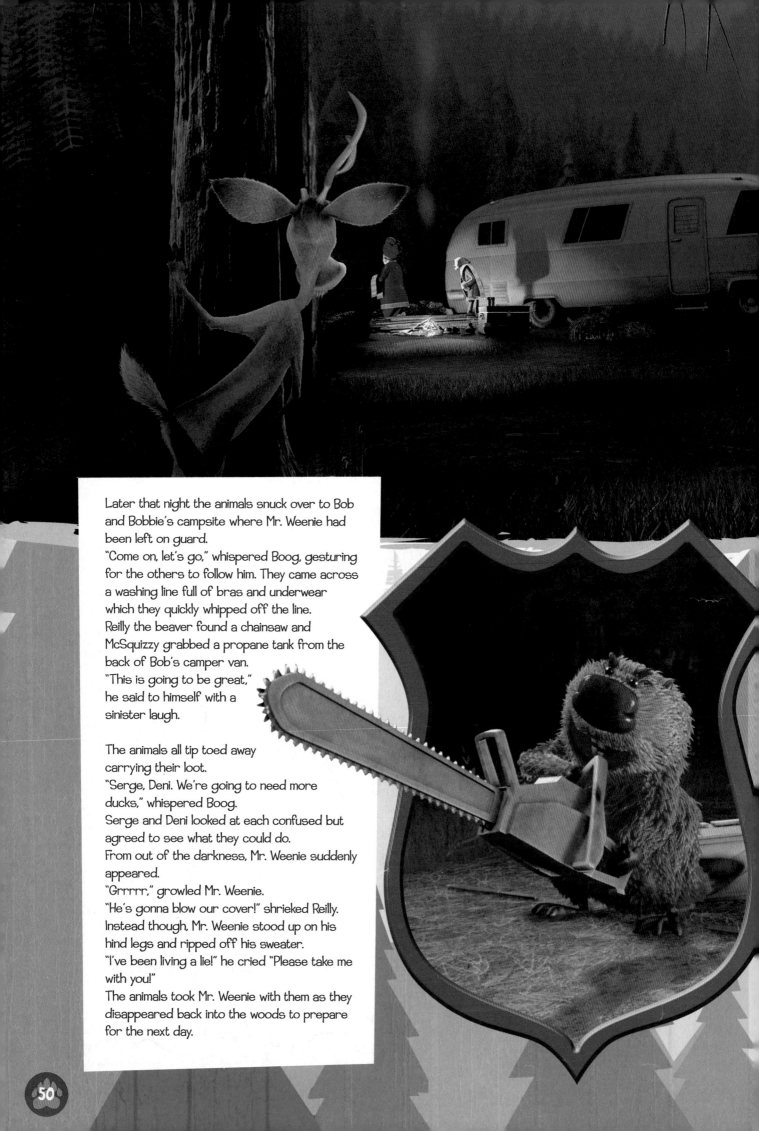

Later that night the animals snuck over to Bob
and Bobbie's campsite where Mr. Weenie had
been left on guard.

"Come on, let's go," whispered Boog, gesturing
for the others to follow him. They came across
a washing line full of bras and underwear
which they quickly whipped off the line.

Reilly the beaver found a chainsaw and
McSquizzy grabbed a propane tank from the
back of Bob's camper van.

"This is going to be great,"
he said to himself with a
sinister laugh.

The animals all tip toed away
carrying their loot.

"Serge, Deni. We're going to need more
ducks," whispered Boog.

Serge and Deni looked at each confused but
agreed to see what they could do.

From out of the darkness, Mr. Weenie suddenly
appeared.

"Grrrrr," growled Mr. Weenie.

"He's gonna blow our cover!" shrieked Reilly.
Instead though, Mr. Weenie stood up on his
hind legs and ripped off his sweater.

"I've been living a lie!" he cried "Please take me
with you!"

The animals took Mr. Weenie with them as they
disappeared back into the woods to prepare
for the next day.

The next morning at dawn all the hunters were stalking their way into the woods. They were making their way across a log bridge when all of a sudden a deer flew past them high in the sky. The animals had made a catapult out of the underwear they had stolen the night before, and the flying deer was the signal to attack!

Hurtling out of the sky came Serge and Deni carrying Rosie and Maria below them. Behind them were hundreds more ducks all carrying other skunks. They were like a flying squadron.
Once they were over their target Maria yelled "All right Ladies, let her rip!" Simultaneously all of the skunks sprayed their horrible stink right on top of the hunters, driving them out of the trees and into open ground. The hunters were all coughing and gasping for air.

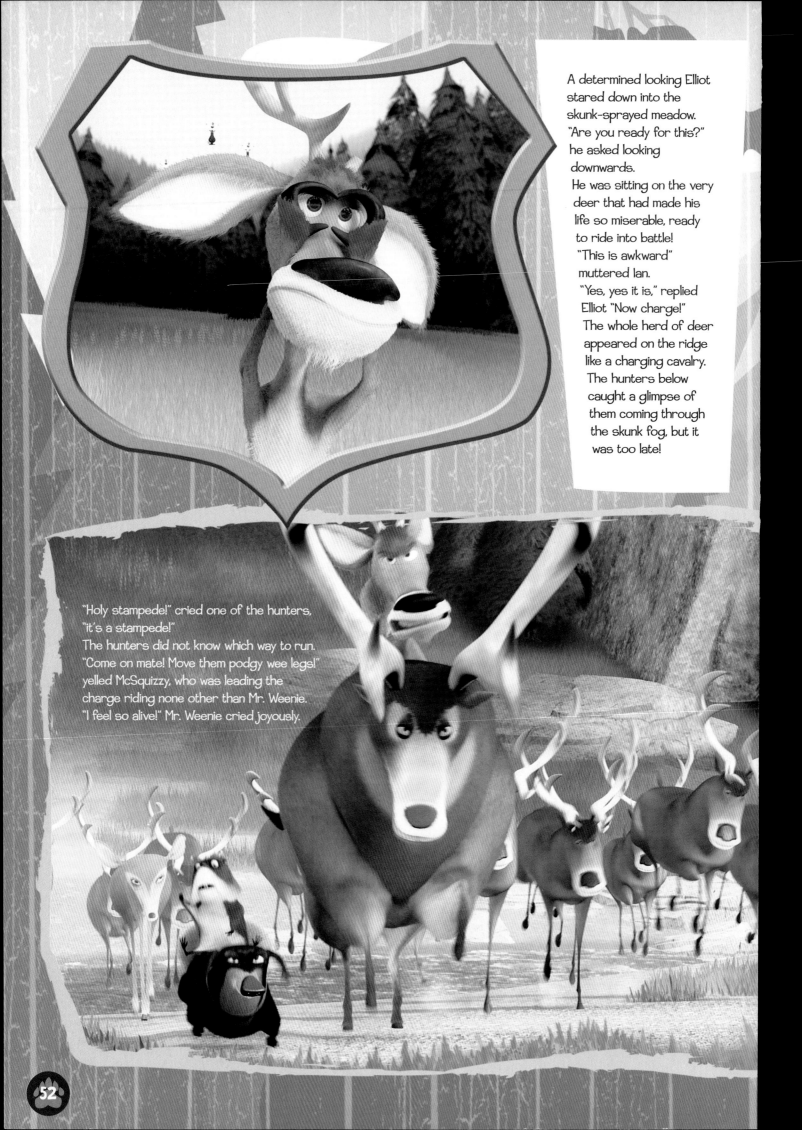

A determined looking Elliot stared down into the skunk-sprayed meadow. "Are you ready for this?" he asked looking downwards.
He was sitting on the very deer that had made his life so miserable, ready to ride into battle!
"This is awkward" muttered Ian.
"Yes, yes it is," replied Elliot "Now charge!"
The whole herd of deer appeared on the ridge like a charging cavalry. The hunters below caught a glimpse of them coming through the skunk fog, but it was too late!

"Holy stampede!" cried one of the hunters, "it's a stampede!"
The hunters did not know which way to run.
"Come on mate! Move them podgy wee legs!" yelled McSquizzy, who was leading the charge riding none other than Mr. Weenie.
"I feel so alive!" Mr. Weenie cried joyously.

Just as Elliot and the stampeding herd of deer hit the hunters from side, Boog and his army charged from the other. Boog was carrying a toilet plunger and a shield as he charged into the fray. "Out of my way!" cried the animals as they attacked the mean hunters, "C'mon let's get 'em!"
In the middle of the battlefield, Boog ran into Elliot, who was still riding around on Ian causing havoc.

"How you doing partner?" chuckled Boog.
"This is great," replied Elliot, "we should do this every year!"
The rabbits from the forest charged at the hunters wielding spoons and forks while from high up in the trees, the Furry Tail Clan pelted them with acorns.
The hunters had had enough and started to retreat.

As the hunters ran back across the log bridge to safety, Reilly the beaver was underneath it sawing away with his chainsaw. The hunter's weight made the log snap and they all fell into the river. Meanwhile, Deni the duck flew overhead carrying the propane tank. The animals had painted a scary face on it to make it look like a missile.

Deni dropped the bomb with perfect timing into the back of one of the hunter's trucks. It exploded with a huge bang, sending the truck high into the air in a ball of flames! Then, one by one all of the hunter's trucks started to explode.
The animals all cheered as the scared hunters ran from the forest as fast as they could. The animals had won! The hunters had fled from the forest never to return.

Meanwhile, while the battle had been raging up the mountain, back down in Timberline, Ranger Beth had heard about all the commotion. She set off in her helicopter to save Boog.

Boog stood in the middle of the smokey battlefield, grinning triumphantly. From out of the fog came the familiar sound of Mr. Dinkelman's music box. Boog strained his eyes to look through the smoke when suddenly he stopped in his tracks. It was Shaw, and he had Boog right where he wanted him.

"Ha Ha! Hello Goldilocks!" snarled Shaw as he pointed 'Lorraine' right in Boog's face.

Shaw laughed and started to pull the trigger. "This is the end!" Boog thought to himself, but just as Shaw was about to fire, a frying pan came flying through the air and knocked his rifle out of his hands. Both Boog and Shaw turned to see Elliot who had just fired the pan from an underwear catapult.

"Bull's-eye!" shouted Elliot.
Shaw screamed and turned to Boog, attacking him like a wild animal, trying to strangle him with his bare hands.
"Quick!" cried Elliot to the other animals, "We need more ammo!"
Elliot started to fire all sorts of camping equipment at Shaw with his underwear catapult but he kept hitting Boog.
"Stop helping me!" yelled Boog.
By now Shaw had picked up his rifle again.
"Quick help me," Elliot shouted as he loaded himself into the catapult.
Elliot flew through the air just as Shaw fired, knocking the rifle out of his hands.

Elliot landed on the ground with a sickening thud. He did not move. Boog's face transformed into something none of the animals had ever seen before, the snarling, ferocious face of an angry Grizzly Bear! Shaw was terrified! His face turned white and he was shaking in his boots. Boog let out a huge roar and jumped on him. All the animals thought Boog was going to eat Shaw but after a struggle Boog leapt up, revealing that he had tied Shaw up and not hurt him at all.

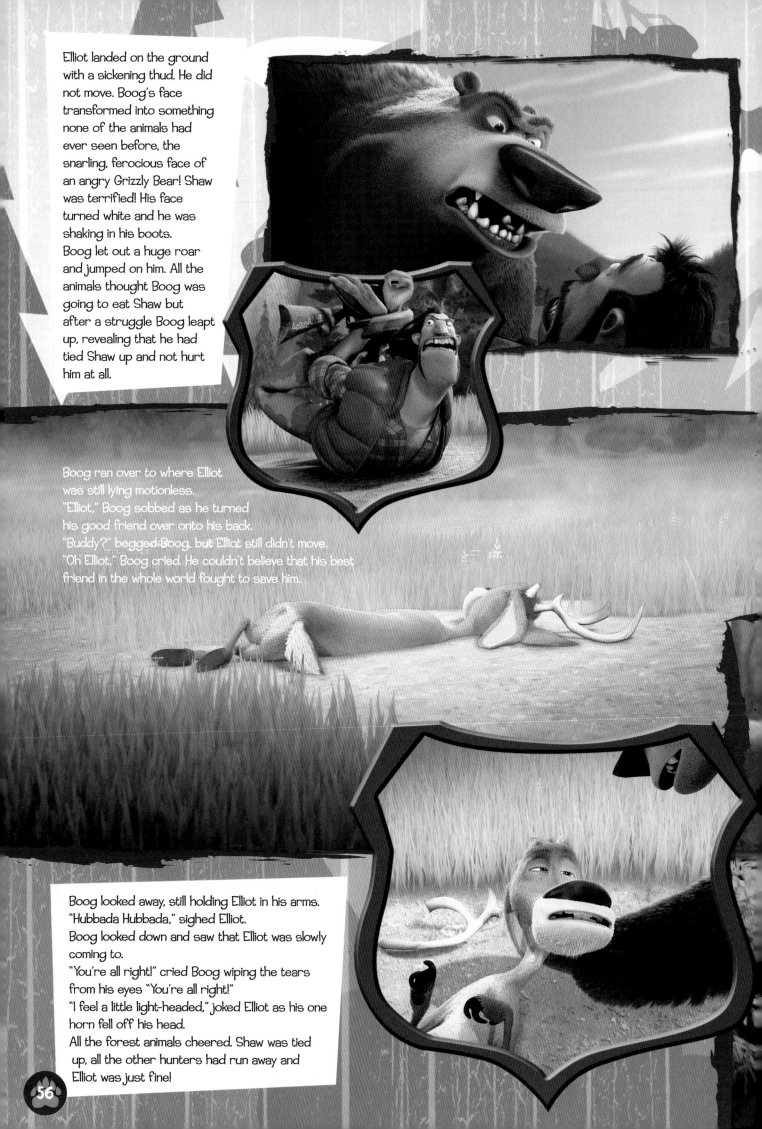

Boog ran over to where Elliot was still lying motionless.
"Elliot," Boog sobbed as he turned his good friend over onto his back.
"Buddy?" begged Boog, but Elliot still didn't move.
"Oh Elliot," Boog cried. He couldn't believe that his best friend in the whole world fought to save him.

Boog looked away, still holding Elliot in his arms.
"Hubbada Hubbada," sighed Elliot.
Boog looked down and saw that Elliot was slowly coming to.
"You're all right!" cried Boog wiping the tears from his eyes "You're all right!"
"I feel a little light-headed," joked Elliot as his one horn fell off his head.
All the forest animals cheered. Shaw was tied up, all the other hunters had run away and Elliot was just fine!

Overhead, Boog suddenly heard a familiar sound. A Park Ranger Helicopter was flying over and coming in to land in the clearing. It was Beth coming to save Boog from the hunters. Little did she know that Boog had been able to take care of himself. All the animals scattered for the forest, hiding from the noisy machine that they had never seen before. Meanwhile Shaw had gotten up and ran for the trees.

The helicopter landed and Beth stepped out. She saw that Boog was okay and a huge smile came over her face. The other animals watched from their hiding places in the woods. Beth and Boog walked up to each other. Beth hardly recognised him. He did not look like the big old pet bear she had left three days ago. Boog gave her a big lick, all over her face.

"Ha-HAAA!" Beth cried as she threw her arms around his big furry neck "Oh, Boog! You're all right!"
"What's he doing?" asked Reilly.
"Is he not going to maul her?" said McSquizzy.
"No, replied Elliot "She's his mom, she's taking us home."

Beth stopped hugging Boog and looked up into his big brown eyes with a huge smile on her face. "Oh Boog, I was so worried. I'm bringing you back with me. Come on, let's go home."
Beth stood up and started to walk over to the helicopter. Boog looked at her walking away and then turned back to look at his animal friends.

They had all been through so much together. He could not leave them behind, but they couldn't all come with him.
Elliot stepped forward toward Boog, hoping to be invited home with him.
Boog looked down at the floor and saw Mr. Dinkelman lying in the dust. He picked him up and walked after Beth.
Elliot dropped his head and looked down at the floor. "Oh no...," he sobbed totally heartbroken. He was losing his best friend.

Boog followed Beth to the helicopter.

"Come on Boog," she said again, "Let's go home"

Boog dropped Mr. Dinkelman into her hands and turned again to look at Elliot. Beth followed his gaze and suddenly realised something.

"Oh Boog, you are home" she whispered with tears in her eyes. "I am so proud of you." She smiled and gave him one last huge hug before climbing into her helicopter and flying away.

Boog walked back over to Elliot and the other animals.

"She's coming back, right Boog?" asked Elliot.

"No, it's just the two of us now, unless you plan on going back to your herd?" replied Boog.

"What? And break up the team! No way. Bros before does!" said Elliot high fiveing Boog.

"It's good to be home," chuckled Boog. Before he knew it, someone yelled "rabbit fight" and the fun started up all over again.

Boog was home to stay.

McSQUIZZY'S

1. WHAT IS A BEAVER'S FAVOURITE FOOD?

2. HOW MANY HORNS SHOULD A DEER HAVE?

3. BOOG LIVED IN A GARAGE, BUT WHAT DO YOU CALL A NORMAL BEAR'S HOUSE?

4. WHAT DO SQUIRRELS EAT?

5. MCSQUIZZY IS THE LEADER OF WHAT CLAN?

6. WHAT IS BOOG'S TEDDY BEAR CALLED?

7. WHAT DOES MR. WEENIE WEAR TO KEEP WARM?

8. WHAT KIND OF ANIMAL IS IAN?

9. WHAT DO THE SQUIRRELS THROW AT BOOG?

10. WHAT DO YOU CALL A BABY BEAR?

QUIZZY

SO WHAT HAVE YOU LEARNT ABOUT THE FOREST AND ALL THE CREATURES THAT LIVE IN IT? BOOG LEARNT A WHOLE LOT: NEVER INSULT A SKUNK UNLESS YOU WANT TO GET SPRAYED, DON'T TOUCH ONE OF MCQUIZZY'S TREES AND PINE CONES ARE NOT AS NICE TO EAT AS WOO HOO BARS. Why not take this quiz and see if you know more about the woods than he does?

11. WHAT DOES IAN SAY "BOOG" IS SHORT FOR?

12. WHERE DOES RANGER BETH LIVE?

13. WHO HIT ELLIOT WITH HIS TRUCK?

14. WHO ARE MR. WEENIE'S OWNERS?

15. WHAT DOES ELLIOT THROW AT BOOG'S WINDOW TO WAKE HIM UP?

16. WHO FORCED ELLIOT OUT OF HIS HERD?

17. WHO IS THE CONSTRUCTION FOREMAN AT THE DAM?

18. WHAT KIND OF ANIMAL ARE SERGE AND DENI?

19. WHAT ARE THE NAMES OF THE TWO SKUNKS THAT SPRAY BOOG?

20. WHO IS THE MOST BEAUTIFUL DOE IN THE FOREST?

TIMBERLINE

PARK PA

PAGE 21

PAGE 60/61

WORD SEARCH

OPEN SEASON

PAGE 34

1. WOOD
2. 2
3. A DEN
4. NUTS
5. THE FURRY TAIL CLAN
6. MR. DINKELMAN
7. A JUMPER
8. A BUCK DEER
9. ACORNS
10. A CUB